THE BIG SWIM

THE BIG SWIM
CARY FAGAN

GROUNDWOOD BOOKS

HOUSE OF ANANSI PRESS

TORONTO   BERKELEY

Text copyright © 2010 by Cary Fagan
Published in Canada and the USA in 2010 by Groundwood Books

Groundwood Books / House of Anansi Press
110 Spadina Avenue, Suite 801, Toronto, Ontario M5V 2K4
or c/o Publishers Group West
1700 Fourth Street, Berkeley, CA 94710

We acknowledge for their financial support of our publishing program the Canada Council
for the Arts, the Government of Canada through the Canada Book Fund (CBF) and
the Ontario Arts Council.

**Canada Council   Conseil des Arts
for the Arts   du Canada**

**ONTARIO ARTS COUNCIL
CONSEIL DES ARTS DE L'ONTARIO**

Library and Archives Canada Cataloguing in Publication
Fagan, Cary
The big swim / Cary Fagan.
ISBN 978-0-88899-969-6 (bound).–ISBN 978-0-88899-970-2 (pbk.)
I. Title.
PS8561.A375B44 2010   jC813'.54   C2009-906084-1

Cover photograph by Gordon Wiltsie/National Geographic Image Collection
Design by Michael Solomon

Groundwood Books is committed to protecting our natural environment. As part of our
efforts, this book is printed on paper that contains 100% post-consumer recycled fibers,
is acid-free and is processed chlorine-free.

Printed and bound in Canada

For Adeline Steinbaum and Henry Fagan,
with a nephew's love

1

WHAT WE HEARD

WE KNEW HE WAS A BAD KID even before he showed up. I didn't know where all the information came from, or whether it was true. I only knew that there was a lot of it and none of it was good.

"He once tied a rolled-up newspaper to the tail of a dog. The dog belonged to the head of sailing at Camp Brunswick."

This was Flap Ears talking. Flap Ears had the upper bunk in the opposite corner from mine, the farthest from the door. It was a nice private spot, perfect unless you were the sort of kid who had to get up in the night to pee.

I was that sort of kid.

Flap Ears was a little crazy, so it was probably a good thing that he had a fairly calm place to sleep. The night was moonlit and I could see his arm and one leg draped over the side of his bunk like a spider monkey.

"He lit the newspaper with a match and sent the dog running," Flap Ears went on. "Second-degree burns. They had to put it to sleep."

"I heard it was at Camp Chippewa," said Tex. Single bunk, east wall. "The dog belonged to the head of pottery and they only had to amputate its tail."

"At Camp Birchwood," said Brickhouse, his mouth full of something even though eating in the cabin was against the rules, "he wrecked all the canoes with an ax just before a big canoe trip.

It took five counselors to hold him down and he practically chopped one of their heads off."

"What do you mean, practically?" asked Legs. "You mean he chopped it halfway off?"

"At Blue Water," said Tiger, "he poured orange paint into the cabin laundry bags and ruined everybody's clothes."

"At Camp Moccasin he beat the crap out of a kid for no reason," said Presto.

"That's not what happened at Moccasin," said Carrots. Carrots' bunk was right across from mine. He reminded me of William Holden in the movie *Stalag 17*, about a German prison camp. I'd seen it on TV one afternoon when I was home with one of my stomach aches. Carrots pretty much ran the cabin, with Tiger as his lieutenant.

"At Camp Moccasin," Carrots said, "he stole the owner's Cadillac and drove it into town.

Wrapped it around a streetlamp. After they released him from the hospital he had to spend a night in jail."

"How did he know how to drive?" Legs again. Legs, who wore his glasses even after lights out, had become my best friend in the cabin. "I mean, he's the same age as us, right? I don't know how to drive."

"You barely know how to walk," said Tiger.

"Anyway," said Carrots, "he would have gone to reform school if his old man hadn't paid off the owner of the car and given a big donation to the police fund. He's always paying out money like that."

"It's a good thing he's goddamn rich," said Brickhouse.

"Maybe it's *because* he's rich," said Presto. "I hear his house has a pool table *and* a Ping-Pong table *and* a movie theater."

"Or because his mom died," said Tex.

Flap Ears said, "I think lighting a dog on fire is a lot worse than wrecking a car."

Legs said, "I'm going to pray that he isn't put in our cabin." He started chanting in Hebrew. It sounded like the portion he was studying for his Bar Mitzvah.

"If you're going to pray," said Carrots, "you'd better pray to the Great Klopschitz."

Old Man Klopschitz was the owner of Camp White Birch. He drove everywhere in a Jeep, the only person allowed to have a vehicle on camp property. He was hugely fat and practically bald, wore sunglasses and white suits, wheezed when he walked and always sucked on a cigar. He'd never taken the slightest notice of me but I was afraid of him anyway.

At that moment the cabin door opened and a beam of light ran across the bunks.

"Quiet down in there."

It was Jerry, our counselor, who was on night duty. Brickhouse said all the counselors hated night duty because they couldn't make out with their girlfriends.

The door closed again. Darkness. Stirring noises as bodies turned over, faces pressed into pillows. I felt as if I needed to pee, but I didn't want to get up.

Legs whispered, "I heard he's a good swimmer. Best in his school. Maybe he'll do the Big Swim."

I hadn't spoken a word, but now I said, "It can't be true. Not all of it. Not about one person."

"Believe me, Pinky, it's true," Carrots whispered back.

After that nobody else spoke, and soon the sounds of sleeping came from the bunks around me.

2
NOT TO BE THE WORST

MY GOALS BEFORE COMING TO summer camp had been modest. First, to survive. Second, not to be hated. Third, not to be the worst at anything.

I wasn't promising camp material. I got frequent stomach aches that the family doctor said were on account of an "anxious disposition," meaning they were all in my head. I hated sports and preferred to either hang around with my two older brothers or write strange stories in my notebooks.

Summer had always meant spending long, free days with my brothers, building balsa-wood airplanes, swimming at the YMHA on Bathurst Street, developing photographs in the basement bathroom.

But this summer they were old enough to get summer jobs. My oldest brother even had a girl-friend. Both the girlfriend and the jobs seemed like a betrayal, made worse by the fact that my parents wouldn't let me stay home by myself.

I argued that going to camp might be a psy-chologically crippling experience, especially if I turned out to be the only kid who didn't know how to stern a canoe down a waterfall, or start a fire in a downpour, or wrestle a Mississauga rattlesnake into submission. I might end up with such damaged self-esteem that I would need a psychiatrist for the rest of my life. Or die of a snake bite.

"Where did you learn to talk such nonsense?" my mom replied. "You're a perfectly normal boy, Ethan. You just need to come out of your shell a little."

I said, "Anyway, I won't be alone. Mom will be home."

Which was when my father spoke up. "I'm taking your mother to Europe. It'll be our first holiday alone in years."

"I want to go to Europe, too!" I shouted, as if it had been my lifelong dream. "I want to see the Eiffel Tower and the Leaning Tower of Pisa and the Taj Mahal."

"The Taj Mahal is in India."

And so on the first day of July, I watched as a duffel bag containing all my worldly goods was hurled into the storage compartment of a bus. I kissed my parents goodbye, barely holding back tears, staring into my mother's own stricken eyes to make things worse for her. Then I shuffled away, head down, into the bus, joining the crowd of kids tussling over seats and screaming at friends they hadn't seen since last summer.

I took a free seat just as the doors whooshed closed. The bus driver blasted his horn, and as we pulled out, everyone started singing the Camp White Birch song.

Everybody but me.

3

HORNSBLOOMER OF THE WILLOWDALE HORNSBLOOMERS

While the campers and counselors were singing their lungs out, the boy in the seat next to me turned and shouted into my ear.

"I'm Leonard Hornsbloomer. Of the Willowdale Hornsbloomers. That's a joke. What cabin are you in?"

That's how I became friends with Leonard, otherwise known as Legs because of the way he would bump into even stationary objects like trees and tetherball poles.

It was because of Leonard that I fulfilled one

of my camp goals: not to be the worst. Because Leonard was. The worst at canoeing, the worst at rock climbing, the worst at archery.

The only activity in which we tied for last place was swimming. We had swim lessons five afternoons a week in the icy waters of Lake Tanasi, and Leonard and I had the same instructor, a girl named Lori whose freckles would merge into one big red blotch when she screamed at us.

"No! No! Drop your legs and then kick out! Try it again!"

No matter how much we tried, neither Leonard nor I could do the backstroke to Lori's satisfaction. She wouldn't allow us to move onto another stroke, so we had to practice it every lesson until I swore I would never use the backstroke again even if I were drowning.

I did so many lengths that I could have back-stroked across the Atlantic Ocean to visit my parents, who were no doubt having the time of their lives. And because Leonard and I couldn't get it right, we couldn't earn the swimming badge that let us canoe, sail or even go in a rowboat without wearing a lifejacket. All the other kids our age only had to throw lifejackets into the boats, but we had to put on the damp, moldy, throat-choking vests that were, as Leonard said in disgust, like orange signs flashing the word *LOSER*.

It was weird, though. Leonard didn't really seem to mind being the worst. He had been coming to Camp White Birch since he was seven, and even though everyone put up with him, they all thought he was a pest. For one thing, he talked too loud and often became hyper-excited. For another, he'd put his face too close when he spoke and accidentally spit.

Also, he laughed when you didn't want to be laughed at, like when you spilled the bug juice or went *splat* into the lake trying to get up on waterskis.

On the other hand, Leonard could solve in his head any math question we asked him. He would sit down at the mess-hall piano and pour out Rachmaninoff or some other impossibly hard piece, abruptly stopping to make some stupid joke. He'd read all the science fiction books of Isaac Asimov and Robert Heinlein and could recount their plots in intricate detail.

He showed me the ropes when we got to camp. How to make hospital corners on my bed. How to avoid being the last person at the dining table to put your finger on your nose so that you had to take all the dirty dishes back to the kitchen. He told me about the Big Swim, and how the few who made it were treated like heroes, and how exciting it was to watch.

Leonard made fitting in easier, and he made me feel less lonely in those first days when I felt almost all the time as if I might throw up.

And in the end, camp wasn't the Garden of Eden, maybe, but it wasn't Alcatraz prison, either. I liked hanging around the nature hut, with its terrariums of leopard frogs and snapping turtles. I liked arts and crafts, where I made marionettes and used the pottery wheel. And I liked the woods.

Camp White Birch wasn't exactly roughing it. We had electric lights, hot showers, a washroom with a sink and toilet on the cabin porch. But we were surrounded by spruce and maple trees, and the paths were a bed of pine needles that gave off a sharp smell, and tiny wildflowers dotted the baseball field and the grassy spaces around the wooden buildings. Farther from the cabins was a heavily wooded section we simply called the Forest, and next to it was a marsh. There was the lake and the strip of beach.

The nights were silent as I'd never known before. One night, Jerry took us to the baseball field where we lay on our backs and looked up into the darkness. I saw my first shooting star.

My biggest fear was that I wouldn't fit in, but the truth was that I usually got along with people. Teachers liked me. I stayed out of trouble, got my homework done, opened doors for old people. I was a good boy but I was smart enough not to bring any attention to myself.

The boys in my cabin turned out to be pretty good, too, or at least not troublemakers or fighters. Their real names were Marcus, Samuel, Howard, Sheldon, Daniel, Allan and of course Leonard. But Carrots (that is, Marcus) gave everyone nicknames to give our cabin a "sense of camaraderie." Flap Ears wasn't because of Sheldon's ears but from a hat he liked to wear to keep the mosquitoes off. Presto's nickname came from the one magic trick he could do, making a straw disappear up his nose.

I didn't like my own name, but I didn't want to make waves. It came from my blanket. All the other kids had standard-issue Hudson's Bay blankets on their beds, but because I was allergic to wool, my mother sent a non-allergic blanket, and the only one she could find was pink. (My mother insisted it was "rose," but it wasn't. It was pink.) And anyway, I'd been so relieved to get any nickname at all that at first I didn't realize how lame it was.

So I was stuck with Pinky.

4
A HAND IN WARM WATER

"HEY, PINKY, WANT TO GO for a row?"

Supper was over and we were pouring out of the mess hall into the still-light evening. The meal had been Sloppy Joes — ground meat and tomato sauce dumped over a hamburger bun. Eating it had made me nauseated.

"I don't know, Legs. I'm feeling kind of sick."

"Sure, from that slop they just fed us. It was like eating someone else's puke."

"Don't say that."

"Old Man Klopschitz is a cheapskate. He

charges our parents a fortune and then feeds us like we're in *Oliver Twist*. You know what that supper looked like?"

"You already said."

"Yeah, but you know what else? Like leftovers on an operating table."

"You're going to make me throw up."

"Don't be so sensitive. Come for a row," he said, putting on an English accent. "The lake air is just the thing you need, old boy."

"All right. But I'm rowing."

"Naturally."

We followed the path down to the dock, past the office and tuck shop. The water twinkled in the light just like it did on the camp brochure.

The lake was long, stretching in each direction farther than I could see, but it was narrow enough to see the roofs of cottages on the opposite shore.

A little more than halfway was Downing Island, named after a family that had lived on it about a hundred years ago. Sometimes kids called it Drowning Island because of a rumor that a camper had drowned trying to swim to it. Stuart, the camp director, said it wasn't true and if Mr. Klopschitz heard anyone use that name he'd spend the rest of the day on a buffa-lo hunt.

A buffalo hunt, Leonard had explained, was a fun-sounding name for walking through camp picking up trash.

It was to banish the rumor of the drowning that the Big Swim had been started. It was held in the second week of August and only the older kids were allowed to try it. They had to swim to Downing Island and back, surrounded by sever-al boats with lifeguards. It took about two and a half hours, and anyone who showed signs of fatigue was pulled in whether he wanted to quit or not.

Only one or two swimmers made it every year. But the reward was immortality. Your name burned into a wooden plaque displayed in the mess hall.

Tiger had an older brother on the plaque. Tiger was expected to try the Big Swim himself one day, and he always got nervous when anyone mentioned it.

Leonard and I passed the end of the swim area, the canoe and sailing docks, and came to the lowly rowboat dock. All three boats were in. We squeezed lifejackets over our heads and tied them around the back like fat bibs. Then Leonard untied a boat and we got in.

He immediately lost his balance, reaching out and shoving me so hard that I fell, my knees cracking against the floorboards.

"Ow! That hurt."

"Sorry."

A scattering of applause and laughter came from the shore. I looked up to see Carrots and Brickhouse and some others on the next dock watching the two of us flailing around like Laurel and Hardy. On the beach a bunch of girls were laughing, too, although I couldn't tell if they were looking at us.

One of the girls was Amber Levine.

I had noticed Amber on the very first day of camp. She had brown eyes and kind of big cheeks and unusually red lips, and her hair was down to her shoulders and her eyebrows were dark, and she was short. She just looked like a really nice person, like somebody who wasn't a snob and didn't make snide comments behind people's backs, and who smiled easily and liked to laugh. She wore cut-off jean shorts and sneakers and T-shirts with funny sayings on them like NOT FROM CONCENTRATE and EVERYONE IS ENTITLED TO MY OPINION. She had a freckle on one knee.

I thought of going up and talking to her at the campfire one night, but then I was embarrassed that she might have noticed me looking at her, and so I didn't.

And now she was watching Leonard and me acting like idiots in a rowboat.

"You stupid goof," I said.

"Hey, what are you so mad at? Are you going to row this tub or not?"

I put the oars into the metal oarlocks and started to heave them through the water.

Leonard leaned back, his hands behind his head.

"Ah, this is the life. Once around the park, Jeeves." The boat moved like it was going through wet cement, but I kept rowing until we were a good distance out.

Then I pulled in the oars and held one blade over Leonard so that the cold lake water dripped onto his head.

"What the...!"

"Sorry. It was an accident."

"Yeah, and so was the Kennedy assassination. And it'll be an accident when I put your hand in a glass of warm water while you're sleeping tonight."

"What does that do?"

"You don't know? It's an old camp trick. Makes you pee in your bed."

"Don't even think about it."

"Sleep lightly tonight, my friend," Leonard cackled. We drifted in the boat, the voices from the shore sounding miles away. From somewhere on the lake came the call of the loon, a shivery rise and fall of notes. I'd heard it often but had never seen the loon, and the sound made me feel a little lonesome.

I looked over at Leonard, whose eyes were closed while his nose twitched.

"Hey, Legs."

"Hmm?"

"Did you ever like a girl?"

"I hate my sister. She screams if I touch her stuff."

"I don't mean a sister."

"Oh, you mean a *girl*." He opened his eyes and grinned. "You like somebody! Who is she? Tell me. *Pinky likes a girl, Pinky likes a girl...*"

He sang out the words, and although I was pretty sure that we were too far from shore for anyone to make out what he was saying, my face grew hot.

"Shut up, Leonard, before I brain you with an oar."

"So tell me."

"Never mind."

"What did I do?"

I picked up the oars again and started to row, moving us parallel to the beach. The oars made a *plonk* sound as they entered the water.

It was hard to stay mad at Leonard. It wasn't his fault he was an idiot.

"Hey, look," he said.

I stopped rowing. "Don't tell me, it's a mermaid."

"No, really. Over there."

I looked toward the shore. Up the beach, past the row of thin birches, was Old Man Klopschitz's white Jeep. I watched him get out, cigar in his mouth.

A moment later two more people got out of

the Jeep: a man in a suit and a kid. The man kept his hand on the kid's shoulder, as if he was worried the kid might suddenly bolt. Old Man Klopschitz was using his cane to point out the various facilities, but the kid kept his head down the whole time.

After a moment the man in the suit took his hand off the kid's shoulder.

The kid didn't run. He didn't do anything.

Then the man in the suit put his hand on the kid's shoulder again and steered him back into the Jeep, and Old Man Klopschitz got into the driver's seat, and the Jeep backed down the path and out of sight.

5

THE UPPER BUNK

IT WAS GETTING DARK BY the time we tied up the boat, and Leonard was worried that we would be late for evening roll call. He dropped the oar he was trying to place back in the rack and hurried up the path without waiting for me.

But I caught up and followed him into the cabin, catching the screen door with the flies mashed in it as he let it go.

Inside were all the other guys.

Also Jerry and the kid from the Jeep.

"You're late," Jerry said. "Okay, everybody.

This is our new cabin member, Zachary Sapoznik. Zach was at another camp but he's going to spend the rest of August with us. I'm sure everyone here is going to make him feel welcome. The first thing we need to do, Zach, is find you a bunk. You can choose whichever empty one you want. There's one beside Brickhouse over there, another under Carrots—"

"What's with the nicknames?" Zach said.

I had expected somebody bigger, but he had narrow shoulders and was almost delicate looking, with dirty blond hair and long eyelashes.

"All the guys have nicknames," Jerry said. "We can come up with one for you."

"I don't want a nickname."

"Hey, that's cool," Jerry said. I could tell he was nervous, almost as if he was afraid of this kid. Mind you, Jerry wasn't much of an authority figure. He walked like a duck and had bad acne. "Anyway, like I was saying, the first thing is to get you a bunk."

"There's a bunk above me," I said.

I had the lower bunk by the door, but the top was empty. I could see Legs making faces at me, as if to ask whether I'd gone crazy, but I ignored him.

"So what's your nickname?" Zachary asked me.

"It's, ah, Pinky."

"Pinky? You've got to be kidding. All right. I like a top bunk anyway."

"That's settled then," Jerry said. He patted me on the shoulder. "You don't have to unpack everything now, Zach. Just pull out your pajamas and wash kit. The rest of the guys will take you to the wash house. After that it's lights out. We're having an early night. I'm going to check in at the office but I'll be right back. Okay, everyone, move it."

We changed into our pajamas and picked up our kits. I remembered going to the camping store with my mom and buying the plastic soap container, the toothbrush tube, the folding hairbrush—everything small and neat and in its place inside the vinyl kit. Now it was a mess of dried soap and toothpaste and sticky hair, everything jumbled inside, the zipper broken.

We filed out of the cabin and down the porch steps into the dark, but then Carrots, who was at the front of the line, halted.

"Why don't you want a nickname?" Carrots said to Zachary. "We've all got them."

"Yeah, and stupid ones, too."

"What did you say?"

Carrots pushed Zachary, and Zachary stumbled before catching his balance again.

It wasn't like Carrots to be mean, and I didn't know why he was acting this way. Maybe he wanted to prove himself, to show that nobody was going to take his place. Not that it looked like Zach even wanted to.

"Leave me alone," Zach said.

"Maybe we should nickname you Car Crash. Or how about Dog Killer. Or maybe—"

But he didn't get to finish because Zachary punched him in the side of the head. Carrots twisted backwards to the ground, and Zachary jumped on top of him.

I had never seen a real fight before. I'd always thought Jewish kids didn't have a clue how. But now they were struggling in the dirt, more wrestling than boxing, until Zachary got a free hand and smacked Carrots in the nose with a short punch.

Even in the dark I could see blood pour from Carrots' nose.

Jerry arrived. He tried to push the two boys

apart and got kicked in the stomach by Carrots. But he somehow managed to get between them, dragging them to their feet.

The ground was littered with toothbrushes and shampoo bottles. Carrots had blood down his pajama front, and he was holding his hand against the side of his nose. Both boys were breathing hard and trembling.

"Who started this?" demanded Jerry.

"That's pretty hard to say," Legs offered. "I mean, Carrots pushed him, but Zachary threw the first punch."

"Oh, shut up," Tiger said.

"Did anybody outside our cabin see this?" Jerry asked. It was hard to believe that somebody else didn't see or at least hear it, but nobody was around.

What Jerry really wanted to know was, would anybody tell Old Man Klopschitz.

"Just us," Flap Ears said.

"All right." Jerry wiped the sweat from his forehead. "Any teeth loose? No? Let's go wash up. Carrots, take off that top. We'll rinse it in the sink."

We all trudged silently toward the wash house.

I had seen a fight and it was nothing like in the movies. It was clumsy and scary and stupid.

And I'd found myself rooting for the new boy, Zachary Sapoznik.

6
WAVES

THE GENERAL CONCLUSION among my cabin mates was that Jerry wanted to keep the fight secret because he was afraid Old Man Klopschitz would fire him. Zachary's father had probably paid three or four times the regular camp fees just to have his son at White Birch for the last three weeks of the season. Old Man Klopschitz would not want to have to expel the kid and give back the money.

The next couple of days made me wonder whether they might be right. Zachary was the

last person in the cabin to get up in the morning. He would slouch into the mess hall while
everyone else was already chowing down.
Stuart, the camp director who made the
announcements, never made some wise-guy
crack about him coming in late the way he did
for everyone else. *"Couldn't find a clean pair of
underwear, Chapman? No place to plug in your
hair dryer, Greenbaum?"* But for Zachary, not a
word. The camp staff acted as if they'd been
instructed to treat him with kid gloves.

For the most part, though, Zachary was on
pretty good behavior. True, he showed zero
interest in any activity other than free time,
when he would either go to the lake and swim
laps, doing the crawl or the butterfly, or just lie
on his upper bunk, invisible to anyone who
came in. But he didn't refuse to participate in
the scheduled activities, either. And he acted as

if nothing had happened with Carrots. That is, he ignored Carrots the way he ignored the rest of us.

I didn't think he hated us. I just thought that we weren't very interesting to him.

But he was interesting to me, like he was some kind of mystery I needed to figure out. So I would watch how he swung a bat, or I would try to guess whether he would eat the chocolate pudding. There was something even about the way he combed his hair in the wash-house mirror, as if he didn't care how he looked but did care at the same time.

Free time came right after the swimming lesson. Most kids stayed by the water and went swimming for fun, or else sailing or canoeing, but I usually headed over to the arts and crafts or nature huts, or maybe just found a shady spot to read or do nothing.

Leonard came up to me rubbing his hair with a towel like he wanted to rub it off.

"You feel like going for a row?" he said.

"Nah, not today."

"Aw, come on, what else have you got to do?"

"I don't feel like it."

"Then I'll find somebody else."

"Okay."

"Come on, Pinky. We'll throw stones at the ducks."

"See you later, Leonard."

"Spoilsport."

He turned around with a huff and marched off. I veered off to a side path and headed to the nature hut, touching branches with my fingers as I walked.

I saw something move on the path and stopped.

It was a tiny snake, a garter snake maybe six

inches long. It slid over some dry leaves and became still.

I took a step toward it. Another. I crouched down and leaned forward, held my breath and lunged.

The snake was in my hands. I cupped them and ran to the nature hut, careful not to trip. On the porch of the hut were a lot of glass Mason jars, and I leaned down and carefully dropped the snake into one.

It immediately tried to slide up the side and over, but I put a lid with holes on it.

I sat on the porch step and held up the jar to take a better look.

The snake slid up and then fell sideways along the curved glass. It had a sort of black diamond pattern running down its back, with a lighter stripe on each side. Its eyes were large for its small head, while the end of its tail was thin and delicate.

"What have you got?"

I looked up. It was Amber Levine. She was holding a basketball. Her hair was tied back with one of those scrunchie things. She was looking at the jar.

"A garter snake. It's just a baby. Want to see?"

"Sure." She put down the ball and sat beside me.

I held the jar up and she put her hand on the back. Her finger was just touching mine.

"It's really beautiful," she said. "It doesn't bite?"

"A big one could, but it wouldn't hurt you or anything."

"What are you going to do with it?"

"Nothing. Just look at it and then let it go. I don't think it's right to keep a wild animal."

She nodded firmly. "When are you going to let it go?"

"Now, I guess."

"Can I watch?"

"Sure."

I stood up and walked to the edge of the path. Amber came up beside me. Then I unscrewed the lid and lay the jar on the pine needles just off the path.

For a minute the snake didn't move. Then the head glided out and finally the rest of it, moving over the pine needles and disappearing under a fallen branch.

"I love the way it moves," she said. "So graceful. Oh, what am I doing? My cabin's waiting for the ball." She scooped it up, half turned to say, "See you," and ran off.

I walked back to the cabin as if my running shoes were floating off the ground.

Amber coming by at just that moment had been the most amazing luck. To be able to show her that I knew something about animals and that I was caring and unselfish because I wanted to let it go.

I'd never looked that good to anybody before.

I walked back to the cabin, whistling the whole way. I let the screen door slam behind me.

At first I thought the cabin was empty, but then I noticed Zachary's legs dangling over the side of his top bunk. I changed into a T-shirt and jeans, threw my wet bathing suit on the porch rail and slammed the door again, whistling the whole time.

Zachary was sitting up on his bed now. He had an earphone in one ear, the wire traveling down to a portable cassette recorder in his hand.

I didn't know anybody who owned a portable recorder. The closest thing was my father's office Dictaphone, which he used to leave letters for his secretary to type. Zachary's tape recorder was black and chrome and the size of a shoebox, with buttons like piano keys.

He pulled the earphone out of his ear.

"What's happening, Pinky?"

"Not much."

"Where's Legs?"

"I don't know. I don't hang around with him that much anymore."

He picked something off his bed, broke it in two and tossed it to me.

I had to juggle it against my chest to catch it.

Half an O Henry bar.

"Where'd you get it?" I asked.

"I brought a stash with me."

He took a bite of his half and the two of us chewed in silence for a minute.

"Your black eye is fading," I said. I hadn't seen Carrots land a punch during their fight, but the evidence was there the next morning.

"It doesn't hurt so much except when I touch it."

"I'm pretty sure you won the fight."

"Yeah, like big deal."

"You don't care?"

"I don't like getting mad like that. I always feel sick after, like I'm going to throw up."

I thought about what he'd said.

"Did you really do that to a dog?"

"What do you think?"

"Then why do they say those things about you?"

"You got me."

"You sure are a good swimmer." A stupid thing to say.

"Yeah, well, it helps to have an indoor pool. It's the only thing about my house that I like."

"But you have a pool table and a Ping-Pong table and a movie theater."

"A movie theater? Give me a break. I'll tell you what I like best. Swimming in the ocean. Going far out from shore and riding the waves back in. You know, I've been thinking I might try the Big Swim. To the island and back. I hear nobody our age has ever done it. Not that I care about that."

"That would be amazing."

"I guess. One day I'm going to learn how to surf and then I'll live by the ocean with, like, nothing. A shack, a guitar, a beat-up Volkswagen Beetle and a surfboard. That's all I'm going to need."

I could see Zach just as he described it — on the beach, maybe with a fire going, and the moon over the water.

"What are you listening to?" I asked. "The music, I mean."

"Buddy Holly."

"Who's Buddy Holly?"

"He was this rock and roll singer from the fifties. His songs are really great. He died in a plane crash when he was twenty-two. They buried him in his home town. Lubbock, Texas."

"Texas," I repeated, as if I planned to go there myself, as soon as I'd learned to surf.

"He's got the same birthday as me." Zachary put the earphone back into his ear and lay down on his bunk so that he vanished from view.

I thought of not just asking questions, but of telling him something that he might be interested in. Like about Amber, and the luck of her coming by. But with his earphone in he might not hear me and, anyway, it felt too weird.

So instead I reached under my pile of T-shirts and pulled out a spiral-bound notebook and a pen. The notebook was about half full of stories

I'd written, poems, other things that couldn't be called one or the other.

Every so often it came on me, the need to write something down.

Finding Zach alone and having this conversation felt like another stroke of luck, and I lay on my own bunk feeling pretty good about how things were going.

I opened the notebook to the first blank page. Sometimes I wrote my saddest stories when I was feeling good.

7
STINK

"SO, MIGHTY LEADER," Flap Ears said to Jerry, his mouth full of peanut butter and toast, "what's on for this morning?"

Meal times were not a pretty sight. Chewing, slurping, gulping. Half my cabin mates ate with their mouths open. No wonder the counselors needed a day off once in a while.

"A nature hike," Jerry said. "We're going to walk the perimeter of the marsh."

Groans around the table.

"Not the Stink Trail," said Carrots. I hadn't

walked the marsh yet, but everyone said it was like visiting a cesspool.

"Trust me," Jerry said. "It'll be really interesting. With luck we'll see a dozen kinds of birds, turtles — even salamanders. Two years ago we saw a moose. Everyone should wear long sleeves and boots and put on plenty of insect repellent."

"Great," said Presto, making a straw disappear up his nose. "We're going to be eaten alive."

"But tomorrow's the Big Swim," said Tiger.

"So? You're not in it."

"We should be preparing somehow."

"That's right," said Legs. "We could build an altar and make a sacrificial offering for the safe return of our beloved fellow campers and staff who are braving the elements."

"Forget it."

"I can't go," said Brickhouse. "I'm constipated. I mean, really bad. I've got to see the nurse."

"You're going," said Jerry. Then he looked directly at Zach. "Everybody's going."

We were walking to the cabin to change, when Leonard came up beside me.

"Didn't feel like going for a row, eh?" he whispered fiercely into my ear. "Nah, you just felt like hanging around with your juvenile delinquent friend. I saw you in the cabin with Zach."

"I really hate it when you're a pest, Leonard."

"Sure, I was a real pest when you didn't know anyone at camp and I was your only friend."

"I would have made friends anyway."

"You're an ingrate."

He moved away before I had a chance to reply. I was mad at him for saying what couldn't be true because I wasn't that kind of person. But it bugged me.

Rick, the head of nature, joined us and we set out.

It was as awful as everyone said it would be. Maybe Old Man Klopschitz believed that every kid had to endure physical suffering in order to get the full character-building experience of his camp.

We trudged single-file over ground so soggy that my boots got sucked into the slime. Mosquitoes buzzed viciously in my ears and landed on my perspiring neck and found their way under my sweatshirt. Every few seconds somebody slapped himself and yelped. The sun beat down and the marsh smelled like an out-house.

Rick put me in charge of the binoculars. At first I was glad, but soon they dragged heavily around my neck, the strap biting into my skin. I was second-last in line, with Leonard just ahead and Zachary behind.

Rick enthusiastically pointed out the fourth

redwing blackbird, muskrat droppings, the leathery head of a snapping turtle that might as well have been the waterlogged end of a branch.

No one cared. No one had the energy even for a stupid joke.

A mosquito landed on my cheek and I slapped myself, coming away with a bloody splotch on my hand. All I could think about was getting back to dry land and collapsing on my bed.

Ahead of me, a dozen mosquitoes clung to the back of Leonard's damp shirt. I had a sudden panicky feeling that the back of my own shirt was just as covered, so I twisted around, trying to see.

And saw that there was no Zachary.

I stopped and stared. No sign of Zachary at all. Had he gotten sucked down into the slime?

Only slowly did I understand that he had gone his own way.

Of course he had.

I hurried to catch up with the others, almost losing a rubber boot.

When I reached Leonard I tapped him on the shoulder. The mosquitoes on his back didn't move.

"Leave me alone."

"Zachary's gone."

"Are you serious?"

"Shh!"

Leonard stopped and turned. "I can't believe it. He's gone AWOL."

"Huh?"

"Like in the army. Absent without leave. They put you in front of a firing squad for that."

"Keep walking," I said, shoving him forward.

"We've got to tell Jerry and Rick."

"No, we don't. We'll pretend we didn't notice."

"That makes us accomplices. There's no way I'm getting into trouble for him."

"Maybe he'll come back."

"And maybe I'm the king of Freedonia. Hey, Jerry! Rick!"

I couldn't stop him. I was sure he was doing it to get at me as much as Zachary.

As soon as Jerry heard, he halted the line. Several mosquitoes landed on my neck, and on the necks of everyone else, and there was a flurry of slaps and yells. Jerry did a frantic search behind us to make sure that Zachary hadn't fallen, shouting his name. He must have been worried about himself as much as Zachary. Who would want to be responsible for losing a kid in a swamp?

We were already halfway round the marsh, and Jerry and Rick began to argue about whether it would be quicker to keep going or turn around. We stood there being eaten alive until Jerry won and we turned back. He refused to consider the possibility that Zach had deserted and insisted that he was lost. Was this another way of pretending that Zachary wasn't breaking the rules?

We marched back as fast as we could and headed straight for the camp office, where we kids stood outside listening to Old Man Klopschitz take a strip off Jerry and Rick. It was hard to know what Old Man Klopschitz was more mad about — losing Zachary in the first place or not starting to look for him right away.

Two search parties were assembled. One consisted of Jerry, the nurse, and an off-duty swim instructor, and the other Rick, Stuart the camp director, and the head of sailing.

There was nothing for us to do but trudge to the wash house. It felt to me like our cabin had become something apart from the rest of the camp, cut off from the shouting and laughing I could hear around us.

Tex scratched at a mosquito bite and said, "I wonder what happened to him."

"He returned to the muck from whence he came," said Leonard.

"I hope he drowned," said Tiger.

"Yeah," said Flap Ears. "Fell down on his face and never got up."

"Do you really think he drowned?" Brickhouse asked.

"It's obvious what happened," Carrots said and spat. It was something he had taken up only lately, and the spit landed on his own boot. "He ran away. He's done it before. He probably went to the main road and hitched a ride into town. I bet he's halfway to Toronto by now."

"I almost feel sorry for him," Presto said. "I

mean about what his dad will do when he finds out. I heard that if Zachary doesn't make it to the end of camp his dad's going to send him to military school in Pennsylvania."

Everyone went quiet. I didn't know anything about military school and I had no idea where Pennsylvania was, but I couldn't imagine anything worse.

Everyone headed for the wash house, but I trailed off and drifted toward the cabin instead.

Carrots was right. Zachary was probably on his way to Toronto, or maybe even Montreal or New York City or that place where Buddy Holly came from, Texas somewhere, so that he could lie on Buddy's grave and listen to his tape recorder.

On the cabin porch I stripped off my boots and socks. There was a line of dried green sludge around my ankles.

I tried to understand why I was so disappointed that Zachary had gone. I'd only known him a few days and we weren't exactly friends. He didn't feel like somebody it would be good for me to get to know.

But he wasn't like anybody else. He had a kind of secret knowledge, maybe, or just a way of being himself that I found both attractive and a little bit scary.

And now I wasn't going to know any more about it.

I opened the screen door and went into the cabin. The place was cleaner than my room at home — beds neatly made, shoes lined up. Jerry was a neat freak and made us tidy up every day.

I sat on my bunk and dropped my chin into my hands.

"What's up, Pinky?"

"Zach?"

His face appeared, upside down, from the

bunk above. He was grinning like a magician who'd just pulled off a trick.

"What are you doing here?"

He disappeared a moment and then slid down the ladder.

"Gee, I don't know, Pinky. Maybe I thought lying on a soft mattress might be preferable to slogging through a swamp."

"But you just can't leave. You can't do whatever you want."

"I don't see why not. I'm not a slave, am I? Old Man Klopschitz doesn't own me. People are always doing stuff because they think they have to. They're training us now so we'll be like prisoners our whole lives. Do this, do that. Live here, live there. I'm a free person, Pinky."

"We all thought you ran away."

"I considered it. But it kind of helps to have somewhere to go."

"They're out looking for you. Jerry and Rick and a bunch of others."

He shrugged.

"What have you been doing, anyway?" I said.

"Listening to Buddy Holly."

"So can I hear what he sounds like?"

"You wouldn't get it. And now that you've found me you'd better go to the office and tell them."

"I wouldn't tell on you."

"They're going to find out anyway."

"Aren't you afraid of what your dad will say?"

Zachary didn't answer. He stuck the earphone back in and lay down on his bunk so that I couldn't see him.

Just as I was opening the screen door he called out to me, "After you go to the office, take a shower, Pinky. You stink like frog guts."

8

GIANT CENTIPEDES
FROM MARS

A COUNSELOR-IN-TRAINING WAS sent to bring in the search parties. They returned swollen with mosquito bites, covered in slime and exhausted.

All considered, Zachary's punishment was unbelievably mild. He was forbidden to attend the Big Swim the next day and then the evening movie. It might have seemed more severe if Jerry had known that Zach wanted to do the Big Swim, but Zach hadn't told anyone except me.

"They had a three-hour meeting and that's

what they came up with?" said Carrots. "Brickhouse got worse for sneaking into the kitchen and stealing a box of cookies."

"And they were those crappy wafer cookies, too," said Brickhouse.

"You still ate twenty of them," Flap Ears said.

"It isn't fair," said Leonard. "It isn't equal justice before the law."

"Yeah, but it's justice before Klopschitz," said Presto. "I bet Zachary's father sent a check for another thousand dollars."

"More like ten thousand," said Tex.

The eight of us were walking toward the beach. The Big Swim had begun more than an hour before and we had seen the swimmers — five counselors, three counselors-in-training and two fifteen-year-old kids from the oldest cabins — dive off the dock to start their swim to Downing Island and back. Surrounding them were three boats, each carrying flotation rings tied to ropes, and rescue poles. Stuart was in the lead boat, with the authority to pull in anyone who looked like he was struggling.

While the swimmers were "killing themselves for the glory of Camp White Birch," as Presto put it, we played badminton in the field and then went on to rock climbing and pottery. Every so often a voice on the loudspeakers announced who was in the lead, who had been taken from the water, how far the swimmers were from Downing Island. When the first swimmer touched a rock off the island, a siren went off.

We joined the rest of the camp for the finish — all of us but Zach, who had to go back to the cabin.

All day I'd been working hard not to care, but now I couldn't resist the tension as the three surviving swimmers approached. We watched as one of them slowed and hovered in the dark water. He was about fifty feet from the shore. We could see Stuart leaning over the keel to speak to him and then a moan went up as he was pulled from the lake. But the last two — a fifteen-year-old camper and one of the girl counselors — reached the shore as a mob waded in to congratulate them.

If Zach was sorry he didn't get to try the Big Swim, he kept it to himself. I didn't think he'd care about missing the evening movie, but I looked forward to it all day because I hoped that Amber would sit with me. I knew it was a slim chance. First, I had to find her. Second, I had to get up the nerve to ask her, and third, she'd have to say yes. But I never got to the second and third, because I didn't see her before we went into the mess hall.

For the screen a white sheet was suspended

from a wooden beam. The projector was set up in the aisle between the seats. There was a ton of popcorn.

It was neat to sit in the dark, the projector softly clacking, and the voices and music crackling through the speakers.

The movie was called *Giant Centipedes from Mars*, an old black-and-white sci-fi horror flick. It had a handsome spaceship captain, a crew member with a secret grudge, a robot named Friendly, a beautiful female navigator and an old scientist who would probably be the first to die.

About halfway through the movie I started wondering what Zach was up to. It couldn't be much fun spending so much time alone in the cabin. He might be glad to see me. We could hang out together like actual friends.

I got up and began to squeeze down the aisle.

When I reached the end, Leonard grabbed my arm.

"You're going to miss the best part. The giant centipede's eggs are about to hatch."

"It's boring."

"You want me to come?"

"Nah, you stay and watch."

He looked at me with an expression that was part angry and part sad. But I kept going, down the aisle and past Lori the nasty swim instructor doing sentry duty.

"Washroom?"

"Right."

"Go ahead."

I made my way along the dark path, careful not to trip over a tree root. Black forms flitted between the branches overhead. Bats. They had spooked me at first, but now I liked watching their jerky movements. One of my favorite things was to walk alone through the camp at night. I took my time, listening to the crickets and feeling the moist air on my skin.

As I approached the clearing in front of our cabin I could hear the faint sound of music. I knew it was Zach's Buddy Holly tape and that he must be playing it through the cassette recorder's little speaker.

I went up the stairs and had my hand on the knob of the screen door when I stopped.

Inside I could see Zachary. And Amber. They were sitting side by side on my bunk with the recorder in Amber's lap. She was looking down at it and Zachary was looking at her.

I backed down the steps.

At the mess hall, I made my way up the aisle in the dark.

"You missed the best part," Leonard whispered as I squeezed past. "The giant centipede has just taken the woman navigator hostage."

9
RAIN

ALONE IN ARTS AND CRAFTS, I was trying to make a guitar out of a cardboard box, a plank of wood and some fishing line.

I wanted to be mad at Zach, even if that didn't make sense, since he didn't know what I felt about Amber. But instead I just felt pathetic for not looking for Amber sooner and maybe even telling her straight out how I felt. I knew that Zach was better looking than me, and a better athlete, and had this kind of faraway look that I'm sure was just so attractive, but it was just possible that Amber might have liked me best if she'd had a chance to get to know me.

But that wasn't going to happen now.

I couldn't stop thinking about it. In frustration I smacked the cardboard box with the plank. The plank bounced up and hit me in the forehead. I screamed out loud but nobody was there to hear me. Right away I could feel a bump rising.

A light rain began to patter on the roof. The patter became a din. There was so much water washing over the windows, it was impossible to see anything outside.

I went to the door and looked out. Campers were scattering down the paths. Puddles were already forming.

I didn't want to be stuck forever in the hut so I lowered my head and made a dash for the cabin, my running shoes sliding in the mud. I was soaked in a minute, but I knew the way so well that I could keep my head down, and then I was on our porch and inside.

The cabin was empty. Everyone else must have decided to wait out the rain. Even my underwear was soaked.

I was just going to change when the screen door flew open.

Amber. She was soaked, too, her hair plastered to her face, her T-shirt to her skin. I looked down at her bare feet. She must have kicked her shoes off on the porch.

"Hi," she said.

"Hi."

"Is Zach around?"

"Are you looking for him?"

"Not really. Well, I guess."

"He isn't here. Were you supposed to meet him?"

"I think so. I'm not sure exactly."

"He can be like that. Vague, I guess I mean."

"Are you a friend of his?"

I thought about it. "Maybe. I'm not sure exactly."

She laughed. "He's kind of hard to get, if you know what I mean. He's not like other guys. I mean, you're easy to understand, right?"

"Oh, sure. I'm totally easy."

"Do you have a towel? I'm kind of drowning here."

"Sure."

My towel hung on a nail by my bed. I gave it to her. She dried her hair, her face, her neck and her arms. There were goosebumps on her skin.

"Thanks," she said, handing it back to me. I just held it as I stood there.

She said, "I hear you write good stories. A bit weird, but good."

"Who told you that?"

"Zach."

"But he's never read them."

"Oops. Maybe I wasn't supposed to say anything. I think you left a notebook on your bed."

"I can't believe he just opened my notebook and started reading. That's my private property."

"He said they were good. Could I read them?"

"I don't know."

Nobody said anything.

"What's your name, anyway?"

"You don't know my name?"

"No. Have you got a nickname, like the other kids in the cabin?"

"It's Pinky. But you can call me by my real name."

"When everyone else gets to call you Pinky? No way. I had a goldfish named Pinky when I was a kid."

"Most people name their goldfish Goldy."

"I know, but when we went to the pet store to get it I was disappointed that they didn't come in pink. Kids are so stupid."

"I know. I used to think that the people in the grocery store had to put the peels on the bananas before they sold them."

"I'd better go. If you see Zach, could you tell him that I came by? Don't make a big thing out of it—"

"No, I won't."

She smiled and opened the door and headed back into the rain.

Only after the screen door shut did I realize that I was still holding the towel.

10
WAR

THE RAIN DIDN'T LET UP, so after dinner we all spent the evening in the cabin. Overhead the electric lights flickered off, on, then off again. Thunder made us jump in our bunks. The guys read old copies of *Mad* or played cards by flashlight, but I just lay on my mattress and went over the conversation with Amber in my head.

I'd thought about not giving Zach the message about her coming by, but in the end I did. He nodded but didn't say anything.

In the morning, a hazy light came in through

the window. We dressed and went out to find a crowd gathered around the charred stump of a pine tree. Lightning had struck it and the tree had crashed, just missing the wash house. Even Zachary came to have a look.

Then Jerry called us aside.

"All right, guys. Today is the day that we've been waiting for."

"We've been waiting for a tree to get hit by lightning?" Flap Ears said.

"No, for a day after rain. You know what rain makes?"

We all just looked at him.

"You dunderheads. Rain makes *mud*. And a night like last night makes tons of mud."

"So?" said Brickhouse. "We're going to make mudpies?"

Jerry sighed. "How did I ever get this cabin? No, we are not going to make mudpies. I want everybody to wear running shoes that can be hosed down after. White T-shirts. The rest you'll hear at breakfast. Now, listen up, cabin. I expect you to be tough. I expect you to be ruthless. I expect you to show no mercy."

"What the heck are you talking about, Jerry?" said Presto.

"Now get to the mess hall. March!"

On the way, we were surprised to see two buses parked on the road to the office. All the girls and their counselors were lined up waiting to climb on. Including Amber Levine, who stood talking to her friends.

Zach went over to speak to her and the two stood aside, their heads close. I looked away, but when Jerry called him I turned back and saw him say one last thing to her before he joined us.

The girls, it turned out, were being shipped out to visit the nearby waterfall, because the planned activity was supposed to be inappropriate for them.

What Old Man Klopschitz had planned for us was a squirt war. He had heard of this game where you filled plastic squirt guns with food dye. Leonard said he was always looking for a program to put on late in the summer that would make everyone want to come back next year.

After breakfast, we were divided up into teams or, as Stuart called them, "companies." Each company was made up of six kids from different cabins. I was in D Company, along with a nine-year-old named David, a ten-year-old named Ralph, an eleven-year-old named Stanley, and two kids who were older than me, Norm and Jack.

The rules of the game were simple. Each company started at a different location on the edge of camp and had to end the game at another location somewhere on the camp's other side.

The more of your company still playing by the end, the more points your team got. Because you were bound to cross paths with other companies, fire fights were sure to take place. The mud was bound to make these encounters "even more fun." You lost two points for every company member who got squirted and earned a point for every enemy player you knocked out of the game.

"If you are hit your shirt will be stained. And if you're stained, you're out of the game," Stuart told us. "Make your way back to the mess hall. There are no other rules. Everything else is up for negotiation, understand? Just use your common sense."

"Squirt war! Squirt war!" we chanted.

Me and my fellow company members hurried to our starting place, the main woodpile. I felt nervous and excited and I knew the others felt the same. On the way we passed three other companies.

"We're going to kick your butts!"

"You're history!"

"Better start writing your wills!"

The woodpile was made of three long stacks of wood, each protected by a lean-to. Here we looked over our weapons — clear plastic handguns with blue liquid inside.

It seemed only natural that Norm and Jack, being the oldest, should take command and work out our strategy.

"Okay, men," Jack said, "we want to win this. But it means being smart and fast. We'll hold to a loose formation with me in front and Norm here covering the rear. Don't waste your ammo by shooting when the enemy is too far to hit. Remember to be as quiet as you can and then to yell like crazy when we attack. That'll strike fear in their hearts."

Our destination was the ski docks, and we worked out a route that took us through the forest, along the edge of the baseball diamond, and between the girls' cabins to the beach.

My position was right flank, with orders to keep scanning the side. I kept my gun close to my body as I moved, just like Jack, who seemed to know a lot about the military.

When we got to the forest I felt relieved to be under cover. But we were only twenty or so paces into the trees when the crashing sound of another company came from our left. Turning, I saw them charge toward us, guns held out, faces ugly.

I had to control my urge to run away. Instead, we all charged, or rather Jack charged and we followed him, yelling like madmen.

We must have been fifteen feet away when the first enemy squirt arced through the air. Then guns were squirting everywhere. Stanley got hit right in the face and yelped, putting his hands over his eyes.

Being on the right, I was protected by the rest of my company and nobody could get an aim on me.

My one shot hit the ground before I slipped on the mud and leaves and landed hard on my butt.

When I looked up again the other company was already running away.

We had two men down: Stanley and also David, the youngest, who had a blue line across his shirt and was blubbering quietly.

"Oh, it's all right," Norm said in disgust. "You can go to the mess hall for ice cream."

David and Stanley trudged off along with the one soldier that Jack had hit who turned out to be Flap Ears.

As he walked away, Flap Ears muttered, "I can't believe I hit a tree. I *killed* a tree."

On we walked through the forest, listening for another attack but seeing nothing. The kid named Ralph tried to squirt a squirrel, but Jack told him off for wasting ammunition. The forest floor was a soggy mess, and leaves stuck to my shoes. I was splattered with mud and my clothes clung to me as I walked.

Twice we heard rustling, and once the shouts and cries of a battle, but we managed to skirt around them.

After a while the ground began to rise and the trees thinned out. Here and there outcroppings of granite and sparkling quartz broke through the ground. A redwing blackbird sang peacefully.

The land rose up to a ridge ahead of us. Jack raised his hand. We halted, crouching low together.

Why had we stopped?

Then I heard it, too. Whispering from just beyond the ridge.

Jack signaled for me to scout ahead, taking my gun so that I could move more easily. I didn't like giving it up, but I slithered on my stomach until I reached the edge.

I could see them kneeling in a clearing

against a stack of wooden flats left over from some drama production. The flats shielded them from the other direction, but not from behind where we were.

I recognized the four kids who remained in the company (like us, they must have lost two), including Leonard Hornsbloomer. It was his voice that rose the most as he argued with the oldest boy. Leonard kept bobbing his head up over the flats, and the older boy kept pulling him down.

I snaked backwards off the ridge to give my report.

"Good work," Jack said, giving me back my gun. "We've got a chance to score some big points. So here's the plan. We crawl to the edge of the ridge. Each one of us takes a bead on the soldier directly below. When I give the signal we rush them. Got it?"

We crawled up the ridge. Jack looked over

and then turned to me and gave me the thumbs up. It was just as I had said.

Jack raised his hand and pointed.

Go!

Scrambling to our feet, we hurled ourselves over the ridge. My heart pounded in my chest. I went over on my ankle but recovered. My own target was Leonard, my former best friend.

We weren't halfway down the hill when the youngest boy looked up and spotted us. His eyes widened but he froze, unable to speak. Leonard noticed him and looked our way.

"Sneak attack!"

We screamed for blood. Norm fired first, even though he was at least twenty feet away. But his stream arched up and came down — *splooch* — on the oldest kid's shoulder. They started squeezing their triggers but, shooting up the hill, their streams fell short. I saw a blue streak cut across the pant legs of the youngest kid. I tried to aim at Leonard, but he was scrambling over the top of the flats and I couldn't get a shot before he dropped behind them.

Heaving for breath, we pulled up before the flats. I hadn't seen their third member get hit in the back as he tried to climb, too, but I'd heard him swear. None of us had been hit, while their whole company had been wiped out except for Leonard, who was cowering behind the flats.

"All right," Jack called to him, "come out of there."

Slowly Leonard rose with his hands in the air. "Don't shoot me."

"Prisoners aren't worth points," Norm said. "Go ahead, Pinky. Plug him."

But I hesitated. It seemed too mean just to squirt him like that and, besides, I knew that Leonard would hold it against me.

"Maybe," I said, "we could let him join our company."

Jack looked at me. "That isn't in the rules."

"Remember what Stuart said? Everything else can be negotiated. That means we can make deals. If Leonard joins we'll be back up to five men. He's worth two points to us alive but only one dead."

"Pinky's got something there," Norm said.

"Yes, yes!" Leonard pleaded. "And I'll be one more gun at your side."

"Come on, then," Jack said.

As we began to move again, Leonard took up a place behind Jack and Norm like he was third-in-command. Jack and Norm began figuring out our point score and talking in low voices about our chances of winning.

We snuck between the deserted girls' cabins and then headed for the beach. All we had to do now was follow the shoreline to the ski dock. I could hear other skirmishes going on, but none was nearby. Somehow we had managed to slip past most of the other companies.

"Halt," Jack called. "What's this?"

Somebody was sitting on a turned-over canoe. He was facing the lake, the low sun a halo around his body. Now I could hear him, humming under his breath.

Zachary. Not only humming but lightly beating the rhythm on the canoe. His squirt gun lay on the sand.

The five of us stood there looking at him.

"This could be a trap," Jack whispered. "Keep on the lookout, men. Approach with caution."

Slowly we moved toward Zach, squirt guns at the ready as we watched out for an ambush. But nobody else was around. We got so close that he must have heard us but he still didn't turn around. So we went around to face him.

"Hey," Jack said. "What's up with you?"

"Nothing." He kept beating on the canoe.

"Where's your company?"

"Funny thing, I seem to have lost them."

"A deserter," Norm said.

Zachary stopped drumming. "I think of myself as a conscientious objector."

"What does that mean?" Jack asked.

I said, "It means he doesn't believe in war."

"But you beat the crap out of Carrots," Leonard reminded him.

No reply.

"You're a hippie," Jack said.

"I'm not a hippie. I'm not anything."

"Jeez," Stanley said, lowering his gun. "What do we do with him?"

"Squirt him," Leonard said. "He's still worth a point in the game."

"But he doesn't want to play," I said. "Just leave him alone."

"He *has* to play," said Leonard.

"I don't know," Jack said. "Seems too cold-blooded just to squirt an unarmed person if he isn't even trying. What do you think, Norm?"

"Maybe if we took him prisoner—"

A blue stream hit Zachary in the stomach. It made a widening stain on his shirt.

"You're dead," Leonard said.

"No kidding."

I stared at Leonard, his squirt gun still pointed at Zach. He stared right back at me and didn't blink.

Only when Jack told us to fall out did we look away from one another.

We continued along the beach. I walked along with the squirt gun hanging by my side. I didn't look out for enemy soldiers.

11
THE BEAR

I DIDN'T SPEAK TO LEONARD for the rest of the day. I knew it was me who was refusing to talk, even though I could tell by the way he deliberately turned away with a snort that he wanted to pretend it was the other way around.

Now I understood that the only reason he had been nice to me at the start of camp was because he wanted to capture me before I saw what a loser he was.

Just before dinner the squirt-war awards were given out (we came in second but I didn't care), and then the buses arrived with the girls. After dinner we lined up at the tuck shop to get our weekly allotment of chocolate bars and candy, and then I went back to the cabin looking for Zachary.

But he wasn't there. Only the tape recorder lying on his bunk.

I wanted to listen to Buddy Holly but I didn't have the nerve, so I went out again and wandered down to the docks, hoping that I might see Amber somewhere. But maybe she was with Zachary because I didn't see her, either, only Leonard out in a rowboat with Stanley, the younger kid from our company in the squirt war. I didn't want Leonard to see me, so I turned back up.

All I knew was that everybody seemed to have somewhere to go but me. I wasn't like Zachary. If he was alone it was because he wanted to be.

I'd never felt more sorry for myself than I did

trying to get that hour to pass as the sun finally went down.

People began to go by me on their way to the bonfire beside the baseball diamond. I got to the fire pit where the logs were already burning and kids and counselors were sitting on bark-stripped logs that formed a rough hexagon around the flames. Smoke and sparks rose up.

I could see some of my cabin mates on the other side, and Zachary, too, with Amber sitting beside him. A couple of counselors were playing chords on their guitars, and people were singing "The Circle Game."

Stuart got up to throw another couple of logs onto the fire, causing a shower of sparks to rise.

"I could tell 'The Monkey's Paw,'" he said.

Groans. "We already heard that story," Flap Ears said.

"Well, does anybody else have a story to tell?"

There was just the popping noise from the new logs.

Almost against my will, I spoke up.

"I have a story." People turned to look at me. "It isn't a story, actually, because it's true."

"Stand up and tell it," Jerry said, motioning with his hand for me to get up. "And speak louder."

I stood up. It felt weird to have everyone looking at me, so I stared at the fire.

"This happened at a camp, but I can't remember the name. There was this kid. There was nothing special about him and nobody paid any attention to him. So one night this kid, he wakes up and can't go back to sleep. He gets out of bed and walks past the other guys asleep in their bunks and puts on his shoes and goes outside. It's this really beautiful night, a million stars up high and the trees looking all silvery, and the air is warm, so he walks along a path, not going anywhere special.

"And then he hears something. This scuffling and snorting noise. And he sees something moving up ahead.

"A bear. But not just any bear. The biggest bear he's ever seen. Bigger than he thought bears could ever get.

"And then the bear hears him. It turns around. It looks at him. And then it stands up on its hind legs. And it is very, very big."

"Oh, man," said Tiger from the other side of the fire.

"The bear looks at him with its small black eyes and the kid sees that something is wrong with it. The way it's kind of weaving its head back and forth. And holding its mouth open. And dripping from its teeth. And he thinks, this bear has rabies. And now he's even more scared.

"But the bear doesn't attack him. Instead it

walks on its four enormous paws up the wooden stairs of one of the girls' cabins."

Three or four people whispered. I went on.

"The bear starts to rub its gigantic head against the door, up and down, up and down. And then it begins to kind of whack the side of its face against the door, like it doesn't hurt or anything. And from inside the cabin the kid hears a scream. And then others are screaming, too.

"The kid knows he has to do something, but what? He looks around and finds a rock. It's about the size of a fist. He throws it. The rock bounces against the bear's shoulder and the bear roars and turns around. The kid starts running down a path. He looks behind him and sees the bear following. He runs faster than he's ever run in his life. He runs like crazy, jumping over rocks, ducking branches. His lungs hurt but he keeps running. He knows that he can't outrun a bear. He heads for the camp entrance. Passes the big wooden sign. Ahead is the highway but when he looks over his shoulder the bear is just about twenty feet behind him. It's catching up, growling and snarling, foam spilling from its mouth. The kid reaches the edge of the highway but he doesn't look for cars. He just keeps running. He hears a horn blare and sees lights coming but he runs on, right across the highway.

"And the second he gets to the other side there is the sound of screeching tires and a terrible bang and broken glass, and he looks back to see that a Jeep has run into the bear and spun out sideways. The bear is lying on the road, not moving. And then the kid sees that it's a police vehicle and these policemen get out of the Jeep with their guns pointed and one of them says, 'That's it. That's the rabid bear.'"

I heard a girl near me say, "The poor bear."

"It had to die if it had rabies," said an older boy. "Did he get a reward or something?"

I didn't answer but went on. "The kid watched as the police made sure the bear was dead. They were so busy watching it and calling into their radios that they didn't even notice him walk back across the highway. The kid walked into the camp again. He went back to his cabin. Everyone in it was still asleep. So he got into his own bed.

"In the morning everyone was talking about the bear coming into the camp. The girls were telling how it banged on their door and how scared they were. And nobody had seen the boy throw the rock or lead it away. And he didn't say anything. He kept it to himself. He stayed the same, ordinary kid nobody really noticed."

I sat down again.

Stuart said, "Thank you for sharing that with us, Pinky. I think I've heard that story. But it happened out in British Columbia, not any-where near here. So nobody has to worry about bears. Now let's have some hot chocolate."

Cups were passed around and we had cookies and then the cups were gathered up again and then a couple of the counselors doused the fire and everyone headed back to their own cabins.

As I was walking, Amber came up beside me.

"I don't think I'm going to sleep tonight." Then she went to join the other girls in her cabin.

I got into my pajamas and then went over to the wash house to brush my teeth.

Just as I was leaving, Leonard came in.

He put his face near mine and hissed into my ear, "If he never told anyone, then how do you know about it?"

I didn't answer. I just walked away from the light over the door of the wash house and toward the dark path that led back to the cabin.

12
THE FIX

THERE WERE ONLY FOUR DAYS left of camp and a change in the feeling of everything we did. Sort of sad but also exciting that we'd be going back to our families, our friends and a new year at school.

You'd think that we would be given more time to do whatever we wanted, but the exact opposite was true. Jerry kept us busy from morning to night, as if he wanted to pack in as much experience as possible. Flap Ears said it was so that we'd go home and talk about all the things we'd been doing and our parents would be so impressed that they'd sign us up for next summer.

Maybe that was why Jerry arranged a baseball game: our cabin versus a team of big, teenage male counselors.

We were getting ready in our cabin when Presto said, "Do you think we have any chance of winning?

"Sure," said Flap Ears. "And Brickhouse is going to stop farting in his sleep."

"Don't sweat it," said Zachary, tying up his sneakers. "We'll win, all right."

Zachary didn't usually contribute to the conversation, and everybody stopped whatever they were doing.

Carrots said, "So you're expecting a goddamn miracle." It was the first time he'd spoken to Zachary since their fight.

"We won't need a miracle. The game is fixed. I've seen it at every camp I've gone to. The counselors will show off for the girls, score some runs, goof around, and then at the last minute let us win. And we're supposed to feel good about it, like we really beat them. It's totally pathetic."

Zachary's words had the ring of truth. We picked up our gloves and walked to the baseball diamond.

Did they really think we were that stupid?

Yes, apparently they did. The game played out exactly as Zachary had predicted. For the first three innings, the counselors ran us into the ground. They hit grounders, fly balls, home-run smashes. They flew around the diamond, stole bases, slid home. Watching and cheering was a crowd of girl counselors and some of the other campers, including Amber.

Then they started goofing off, wearing their gloves on their heads, pretending to bang into one another. Jerry even dragged second base along with his foot, so he'd stay safe.

And in the last two innings we began to score

runs. Jerry, taking his turn on the mound, lobbed us soft pitches that were easy to hit. Even Leonard hit one past second base. In the field, the counselors fumbled the ball so we could keep running.

Pretty soon we were winning.

We were lining up in batting order when Carrots said, "Zach was right. We look like a bunch of jerks."

Carrots walked to first base, and it was Zach's turn to bat.

"You going to do something?" Presto asked him as he headed for the plate. "Tell them what we think?" But Zach didn't answer so we all just watched. Would he refuse to swing the bat? Would he say something? Would he turn and walk away from the diamond, something that none of us had the nerve to do?

Zach had a chance to make things right with the whole cabin, including Carrots. To stand up for all of us.

And what did he do? He took his stance, waited for the pitch, and hit the ball. He ran to first, saw the outfielder deliberately fumble over it, and headed for second. The counselor at second, a beefy guy named Lou who probably meant to go the other way, stepped right into Zach as he was making for the base. Zach grunted as he went over Lou's hip, landing in the dust. He got up, brushed himself off and limped back to the base.

He didn't say a word.

Carrots shook his head as he picked up the bat.

After lunch came swimming, free time, archery, arts and crafts, dinner (with a special dessert — ice cream in little paper cups), and then a production of *Grease* by the oldest kids. Zach came to everything, limping from his collision during the baseball game. When he put his bathing suit on, I saw the bruise on his leg.

During free time, he and Amber took a canoe

out on the lake and disappeared behind the trees along the shore.

After dark, the temperature dropped. Jerry made us take showers and we shivered as we made our way back to the cabin. In bed, I lay with my legs curled up, the sheets still icy.

"I don't get it," Carrots said into the dark. We all knew who he was talking to. "Why didn't you do something? You knew it was fixed but you played the game anyway."

Silence for a moment. "Because I didn't feel like it."

"I know why," Leonard said. "It's obvious. Because camp is almost over. You only have to last three more days. There isn't any point in ending up at military school just for a stupid ball game."

"Whatever," Zachary said.

I thought Leonard was right, but I was too tired to think about it anymore. I couldn't fight sleep.

13

A REALLY, REALLY BAD IDEA

SOMEBODY BEGAN SHAKING MY shoulder, dragging me up from the bottom of a deep well.

"Wake up. Come on, Pinky, open your eyes."

"What? Is something wrong?"

"I need your help. Get dressed."

I sat up mechanically and stared at the dark forms sleeping all around me. Zachary was kneeling by my bed, already dressed.

"What time is it?" I said.

"I don't know exactly. Around two. Now come on, here are your pants."

I began to pull my jeans up over my pajamas.

"Why are we getting up? We're going to get in real trouble."

"Not if you keep your voice down. Let's go."

I put on my sneakers and followed Zachary out the door, careful not to let it slam.

It was chilly out, and I wished I'd put on a jacket. Zachary was walking quickly down the path, even with the limp from his bruise, and I stumbled to catch up with him.

"Zachary, stop. We can't go out in the middle of the night. If they catch us you'll be kicked out for sure and then you'll have to go to that military school in Pennsylvania. Camp's almost over. Don't screw up now."

"I'm not going to screw up. Come on."

He continued down the path, creeping past the girls' cabins and down to the beach. We walked past the docks until we got to the rowboats.

He picked up a lifejacket and pushed it into my arms.

"Put it on."

"Okay, but I'm not getting into a boat."

Zachary threw a couple of oars into a rowboat and untied it from the dock. Then he kicked off his shoes, pulled off his shirt and pushed down his jeans.

He had a bathing suit on underneath.

"Suit yourself," he said. "I'll do the Big Swim alone. And if I get tired and drown it'll be your fault."

"You want to do the Big Swim? Now?"

"Yup."

"This is a really, really bad idea."

Zach turned to me and smiled. "Don't worry so much about everything. I liked how that kid in your story rescued everyone from the bear and kept it to himself. It would be pretty cool to have a secret like that. Relax, Pinky. It'll be fun."

"Fun? How could this possibly be fun?"

I heard something, a branch crackling underfoot. My heart jumped.

If it was a counselor, we were fried.

Zach and I stared at the stand of trees above the water, but it was too dark to see much.

Then a figure stepped away from the trees, too short to be a counselor. Even before it reached us, I knew it was Amber.

"Hey," she said as she came up to us. "I've been waiting like a half hour."

"Aw, man, I told you not to come."

"You told Amber about this great plan and not me?"

Zach shrugged. Then he went to the end of the dock and slipped into the water.

Amber looked at me.

"Come on," she said.

We scrambled into the boat, and while she pushed it off with her hand, I struggled to get the oars into the oarlocks.

I looked for Zachary but could see only the dark, shining water reflecting the moonlight.

I stroked the oars and Amber pointed and said, "There," and I saw his head, a darker form against the water.

"Watch it!" he spluttered. "You almost brained me with the oar."

"Sorry."

"The water is like ice."

"Come into the boat."

But he started to swim, doing the crawl, his strongest stroke. I rowed to keep ahead, my eyes always on him. I didn't know what I would do if he started to drown. At the start of camp we'd had a lesson in performing artificial respiration,

but I could hardly remember it. Were you supposed to pinch the nose or not?

Please, I said silently, *don't make me have to
save Zachary.*

At least there was no wind to make the rowing harder. The night was clear, and my senses,
groggy at first from sleep, had woken up.

"He's not going in a straight line," Amber
said. "I think it's because of his hurt leg. He
keeps having to correct himself, which means
he's swimming farther than he needs to."

She was wearing a sweatshirt and a pair of
jeans and sneakers without socks. Her hands
were clutching the side of the boat and she
leaned forward, as if she was trying to help
Zachary swim. But then she let go and turned
around toward me. She looked up at the sky.

"It's an unbelievable night, isn't it? We'll
never forget this."

"I'd like to forget it already."

"Don't spoil it."

"Sorry."

"I hate the last day of camp. I always cry. I mean, I'm glad to be going home. But it feels like I'm leaving the country I belong to or something."

Did camp feel like my country? I didn't think so. Maybe it felt more like a foreign country, and I was finally learning to understand the language.

I wondered if on the last day, Amber would run up to me in front of the buses that were going to take us to the city, throw her arms around me and cry.

That would be something to look forward to.

It was a long time before I could see, over my shoulder, the trees above the shoreline of Downing Island. Zachary had changed his stroke a few times but was now back to a slow and steady crawl.

At last we got to the rocks, where Zachary clung, breathing heavily, his lips purple even in the moonlight.

Now that I had stopped rowing, I could feel the ache in my arms.

"It took me longer than I expected," he panted.

"Just getting here's pretty amazing, Zach. Why don't you get in and we'll row back?"

"That's a good idea," said Amber. "Nobody else our age could get this far."

"I want to do the whole thing." He took a few slow breaths. "You know what I was thinking about? My dad. How if something happened to me he'd be all alone. I never thought about that before."

He let go of the rock, vanishing under water. Amber looked at me with wide eyes and then we both turned to the water. A moment later he came up and started to swim.

"Here, let me row," she said. My arms really ached now and I was glad to change places. She turned the boat after him. Zach looked as if he was having trouble raising his head above the water to take a breath. His bruised leg seemed to be dragging more. He messed up his stroke, bobbed under and came up coughing. When he could breathe again he switched to the sidestroke.

Amber pulled the boat in front of him. She rowed steadily, her eyes always on Zach.

I thought how it was too bad that everyone in camp couldn't know that Zach was making the Big Swim. They could be cheering him on. His name could go up on the plaque.

Slowly, slowly, we headed toward the beach. Zachary was moving at maybe half the speed he had been going the other way.

How long had we been out here? I couldn't tell, but it felt like hours.

Zachary turned over and began to do the backstroke. I could hear his quick, shallow breathing. Amber's arms must have been getting tired because she grimaced every time she pulled the oars through the water.

"Do you want me to take over again?"

"No, I'm okay."

"Amber?"

"Yes?"

Now was my chance. If I didn't tell her how I felt, I never would. It probably wouldn't matter. There was no way I could compare to Zach, but at least she would know.

"Amber," I said, turning toward her, "I just want you to know that I think you're – "

"He's gone under!" Amber cried. "Where is he?"

I turned back and looked for Zachary, but I couldn't see him. Had he surfaced somewhere ahead? I looked but still couldn't see him.

"Zachary!" I shouted.

His head broke the glimmering surface of the water. His arms flailed and he coughed weakly, slipped under, bobbed up again. Amber dug in one oar to turn us around and then maneuvered us alongside him.

I grabbed Zach's wrists. He let me haul him into the boat, scraping his stomach along the side. He lay back on the wooden slats coughing.

"Almost made it," he said without opening his eyes.

Amber rowed hard until her arms were too tired and I took over. She held Zach's hand as he lay there looking like he was asleep.

I didn't stop until the pointed bow slid onto the sand of the beach. Now we would have to put away the boat and get Zachary back to bed without anyone knowing.

"Hey, what exactly are you doing there!"

It was Stuart's voice. I looked up and saw three silhouettes on the rise.

One of them leaned on a cane.

Old Man Klopschitz.

"Go on! Run!" I hissed.

Amber stepped onto the beach and sprinted off. Somebody shouted at her but didn't follow. I told myself to run but I didn't.

I felt a hand on my shoulder.

Turning, I saw Old Man Klopschitz, cigar in his mouth, leaning on his cane.

"You, boy," he said grimly. "Get out of that boat."

14
COME BACK SOON

STUART WRAPPED ZACHARY IN blankets and drove him to the hospital in Haliburton, in case he was suffering from hypothermia. It turned out that he was only exhausted. Still, he was going to stay in the hospital for twenty-four hours.

I found this out in the morning from a secretary. Old Man Klopschitz let me go to bed after he discovered us, but in the morning Jerry took me to the office before breakfast.

Old Man Klopschitz came in, cleared his

throat of phlegm and said, "You're expelled, kid." Then he left me alone again.

Unlike Zachary, I'd never been kicked out of anything. I'd never even had a detention in school.

The secretary brought me some breakfast because I wasn't allowed to leave the office building, not even to pack my duffel bag. I sat in a room without windows, but I could hear kids outside, running and laughing. I tried to imagine what Carrots and Flap Ears and the other guys were saying.

When the secretary came in to get a file I asked if I could say goodbye to my friends, but she said that Old Man Klopschitz had forbidden my speaking to any campers.

Still no one came.

Finally Jerry came into the room and told me to come with him. I walked outside, the bright light hurting my eyes, and saw my mother and father standing beside our car. The trunk of the car was open and my duffel bag was inside.

I ran to them and threw myself sobbing into my mother's arms. She held me tight and my father stroked my hair and they were both saying, "It's all right, it's all right."

They put me in the car. I didn't look out the windows because I didn't want to see any campers staring at me.

My parents got in and my father slowly drove along the road. A sign nailed to a tree said *You Are Leaving Camp White Birch. Come Back Soon!* On either side of us, branches heavy with leaves or needles brushed our car. We turned onto the highway and speeded up.

"You must be hungry," my mother said. "We brought you some lunch."

Only then did I notice the paper bag on the seat beside me. I opened it and saw a tuna fish sandwich wrapped in cellophane, an apple, a bag of potato chips and a can of ginger ale, which was the drink my mother always gave me when I was sick. I wolfed down the sandwich, which tasted delicious, just the way my mother always made it, and drank the ginger ale.

"Oh, yes," my mother said. "Somebody gave us a note for you. A girl."

She reached back and I took the folded piece of paper from her. But I didn't open it right away. I held it in my hand and looked out the window at the trees going by, the gas station, a pile of old tires, signs for bait and picnic tables.

I opened the letter and read it.

The wind made a sound through the open windows.

I read it again.

"Are you okay back there?" my father asked.

"Yes, I'm okay," I said.

And I was.